For every being who has been lost.
And for Allison, Vincent, and Will, who have found me. –P.O.

For my children, Ethan and Fox. –J.K.T.

Mingo the Flamingo
Copyright © 2017 by Pete Oswald and Justin K. Thompson
All rights reserved. Printed in the United States of America.
No part of this book may be used or reproduced in any manner whatsoever without written permission except in the case of brief quotations embodied in critical articles and reviews. For information address HarperCollins Children's Books, a division of HarperCollins Publishers, 195 Broadway, New York, NY 10007.
www.harpercollinschildrens.com

Library of Congress Cataloging-in-Publication Data
Names: Oswald, Pete, author. | Thompson, Justin K., date, illustrator.
Title: Mingo the flamingo / written & created by Pete Oswald and Justin K. Thompson.
Description: First edition. | New York : HarperCollins, [2017] | Summary: Mingo is injured and loses his memory when he faces a bad storm during his first migration, but he makes friends who will do whatever it takes to help him heal and get back where he belongs.
Identifiers: LCCN 2015018262 | ISBN 9780062391988 (hardcover)
Subjects: | CYAC: Flamingos—Fiction. | Birds—Migration—Fiction. | Domestic animals—Fiction. | Amnesia—Fiction.
Classification: LCC PZ7.1.O86 Mi 2017 | DDC [E]—dc23
LC record available at http://lccn.loc.gov/2015018262

The artists used gouache and digital software to create the illustrations for this book.
Typography by Jeanne L. Hogle
16 17 18 19 20 PC 10 9 8 7 6 5 4 3 2 1
❖
First Edition

MINGO
the Flamingo

WITHDRAWN

Written & Created by
PETE OSWALD and JUSTIN K. THOMPSON

HARPER
An Imprint of HarperCollinsPublishers

Today was the big day! For the first time, Mingo was about to head south for the winter. His bags were packed and he was ready to fly.

The journey did not get off to a good start.
They flew straight into a storm—*boom, clap, thunder, lightning!*

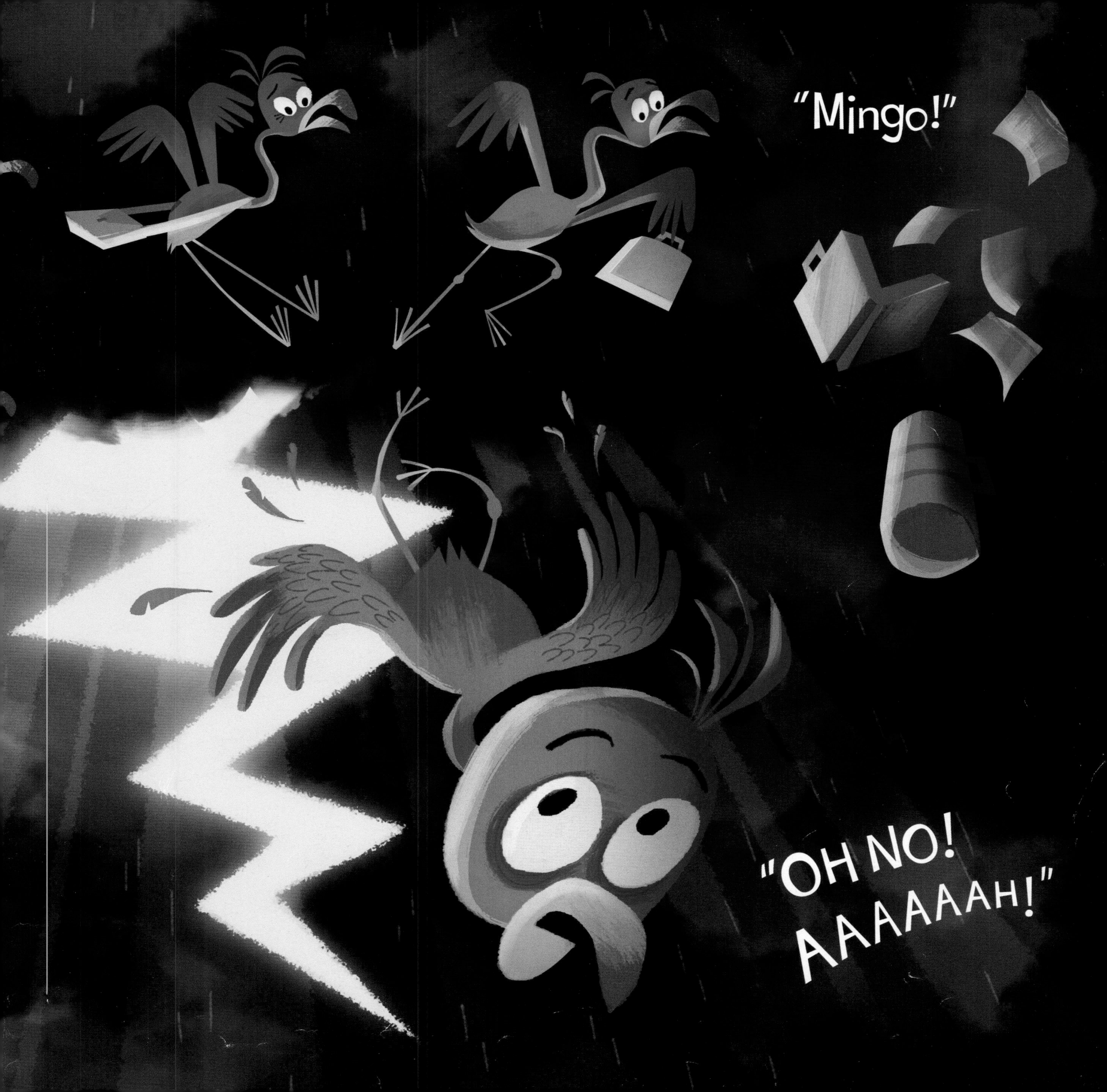
"Mingo!"
"OH NO!
AAAAAAH!"

Mingo flew down,

. . . down,

. . . down!

Mingo had landed in a very strange place.

"You ever seen such a thing?"

"Sure seems strange."

"What is it?"

"A golf club!" said Rooster.

"It's most definitely a mustache," said Goat.

"No. It belongs on the front lawn," said Mouse.

Mother Hen pushed them aside, "No, no, no! This poor baby is hurt!
And I'm here to help. You had quite a fall," Mother Hen said to Mingo.
"Can you remember anything at all?"

Mingo suddenly realized he had no idea who he was.

Nope. Nothing felt right.

"Don't worry," said Mother Hen. "You have
a home until you figure it out. We're a big family,
but there's always room for one more!"

Slowly but surely . . .

he began to feel like he'd been down on the farm forever.

But still, something
was not quite right.

"What's the matter?"
asked Mouse.

Before he could answer, Mingo heard something.

He rushed outside. High in the sky,
geese were flying south.

Mingo shouted, "I remember! I'm a
flamingo! I can fly too!" He turned to
Mouse. "I have to fly home!"

"Slow down, friend!" said Mouse. "Before you take off, you need to get that busted wing into shape. I'll be your personal trainer!"

Mingo ran!

He pulled!

He even did one-winged push-ups!

Soon his wing was stronger than ever. Mingo was ready to take off!

From the top of the barn
Mingo said,

"Goodbye,
everyone!

Thanks for
the memories!"

Then Mingo spread his
newly pumped-up wings.

Three—
two—
one . . .

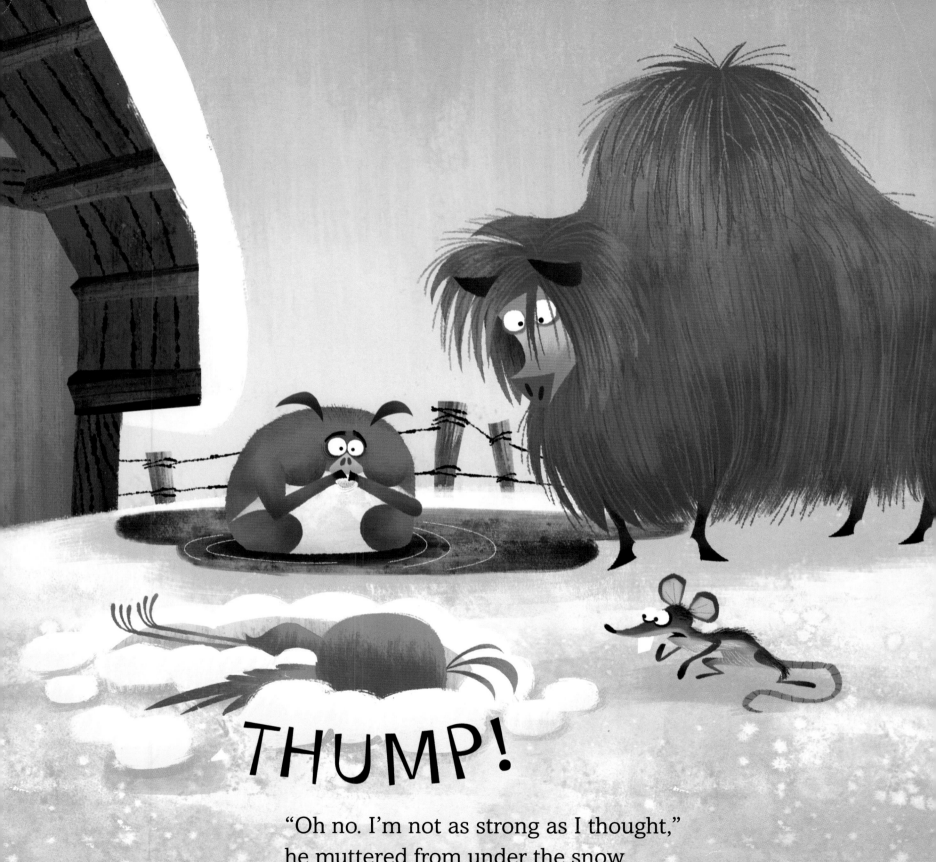

THUMP!

"Oh no. I'm not as strong as I thought,"
he muttered from under the snow.

"I'll never get home again," said Mingo.

But little did Mingo know,
his friends were one step ahead.
They had a plan. . . .

The propellers spun! The engine roared! Mingo took off!

Up, up, up! High into the sky.

After many days, Mingo touched down.

"Mom! Dad! I'm home!"

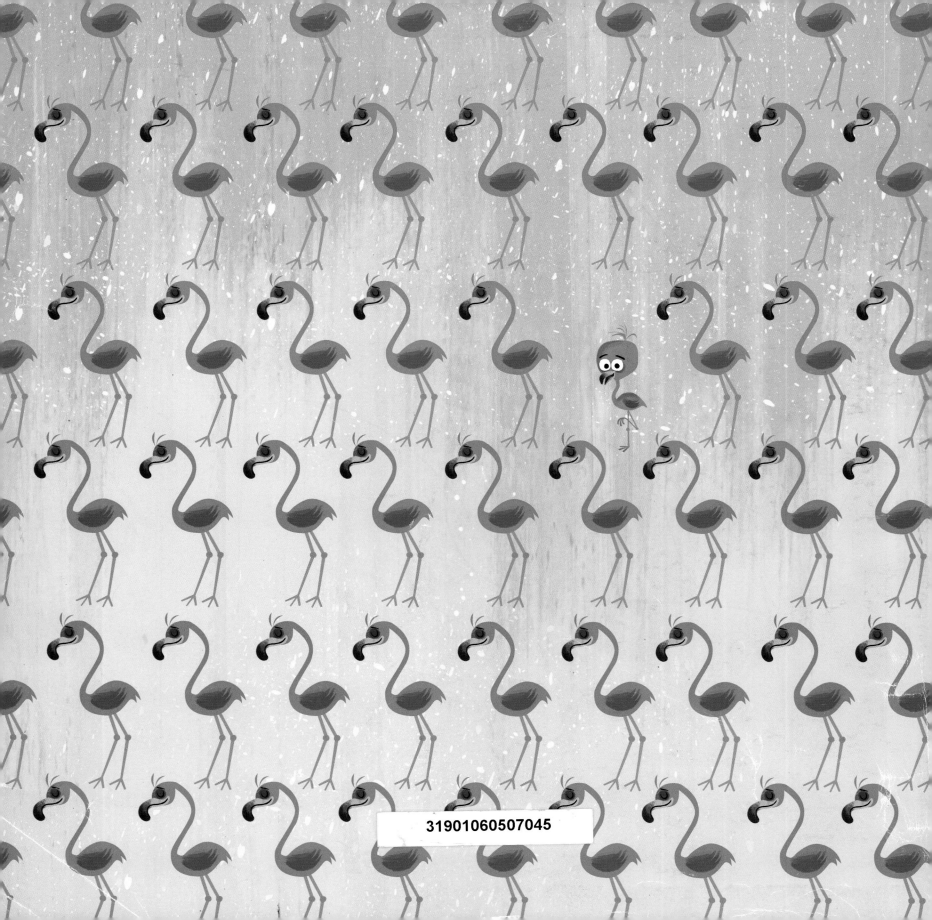